W9-DAX-511

THE
BIG
FIX

BARE KNUCKLE

THE BIG FIX

NATHAN SACKS

darby creek
MINNEAPOLIS

Darby Creek
A division of Lerner Publishing Group, Inc.
241 First Avenue North
Minneapolis, MN 55401 U.S.A.
Website address: www.lernerbooks.com

Cover and interior photographs © iStockphoto.com/Steve Krumenaker (brick background); © iStockphoto.com/tomograf (paper texture); © iStockphoto.com/ Abomb Industries Design (woodrat); © iStockphoto.com/CSA_Images (fist).

For reading levels and more information, look up this title at www.lernerbooks.com.

Main body text set in Janson Text LT Std 12/17.
Typeface provided by Linotype AG.

Library of Congress Cataloging-in-Publication Data

The Cataloging-in-Publication Data for *The Big Fix* is on file at the Library of Congress.
    ISBN: 978-1-4677-1459-4 (LB)
    ISBN: 978-1-4677-2407-4 (EB)

Manufactured in the United States of America
1 – SB – 12/31/13

NEW YORK CITY.
THE 1870s.
THE FIGHT STARTS NOW.

CHAPTER ONE

A passenger ship sailed across the Atlantic, gliding from the port of London toward Manhattan. Some of the travelers on board were immigrants, hoping to escape persecution in their home countries. Others were businessmen, hoping to strike gold in the American West. Another passenger was George Choogart, an eighteen-year-old from the East End of London. He was traveling to America for a job offer. On the thirtieth day of his journey, he stood on the deck of the ship, looking out to sea. He was waiting to see the American continent appear over the horizon. The boat was close to its destination.

George was tall and muscular for his age. He gripped the railing over the deck with his massive fists. Other than the clothes on his body, he carried only two items. In his left coat pocket was a worn copy of Charles Dickens's novel *Bleak House*. George had read the book cover to cover and then read it again over the course of the trip. His other possession was a letter in his right coat pocket. George took it out of his coat and began to read it for the hundredth time.

For: George Choogart, Fleet St., London, England
From: Nelson Jones, Publisher, The New York Times

Dear George:
Your reports on the Fleet Street scandal have made front page news at the Times on at least seven separate occasions. My editors are very impressed with your investigative journalism. We would like to offer you work in New York City. Please take our offer under consideration. We will arrange for boat travel

upon your reply. This newspaper will also provide lodging upon your arrival. Please reply to either confirm or reject this offer.

Regards,
Nelson Jones, Publisher

George folded the letter and put it back in his pocket. He still could not believe it real that he, a teenage Brit, had been invited to join the *New York Times*. He was about to reread the letter for the hundred and first time. Then he heard a voice.

"A feller could hurt his eyes, staring out to sea for so long."

George turned around to locate the source of the voice. Standing behind him on the deck was a Scotsman with messy brown hair, wearing a brown coat.

George had never seen this man. "Have we met before?" he asked.

"Nae likely, sir. I've spent most of the trip in my cabin. Steve Oakley's my name."

"Mine is George Choogart. Charmed to meet you."

"What brings an Englishman to the states?"

"A job in New York," George said.

"Me as well! Right on the Bowery."

"The Bowery?" George had heard the word before but was not sure of its exact meaning.

"The Bowery, yes." Steve Oakley's eyes became wide, as if he were about to begin a story. "The dirtiest, most disgusting, most lively area in the isle of Manhattan. Where the markets are always open and a show is always playing. Where the ladies are as beautiful as they are vulgar, and the gangsters and politicians drink and dance together."

"Sounds like where I grew up." George recalled his poor, desperate childhood in the East End.

"My brother, they call him just Oakley, he told me all about it in letters. He moved to America many years back. He works in a club, refereeing fights. Said he would find me work."

"Fights?"

"Oh yes, every night," Steve said. "Bare-knuckle stuff, very brutal. People come from all over the city, rich and poor, just to see people punch the stuffing out of each other. It's a bloody affair. The rich folks bet money on who wins, while the poor just watch. That's what my brother said."

Steve Oakley reached his hand over to clasp George's right arm. "You're a right strong fella yourself, George. Ever think about making it as a bareknuckle fighter? You'd be a natural."

"Unlikely. I am a journalist."

"A journalist! Now *that's* unlikely. How old can you be?"

"Eighteen, but I started filing at twelve," George said. "Not much choice when you grow up poor."

"I would ask you which newspapers you work for but can't say I'd be familiar. Never learned to read."

"Quite understandable. Many of the smartest people I know cannot read."

Suddenly they both heard an excited voice. It was the ship's captain. "Destination straight ahead!" he yelled, ringing a bell throughout the cabin. Indeed, both Steve and George could now see the faint outline of New York City buildings in the distance. The conversation between them ended for a time as they both stared at the cityscape in wonder. Each man imagined their futures.

Steve Oakley spoke after a moment. "George, you mind if I ask you a question?"

"Not at all, Steve."

"You're a Brit, and I'm a Scot. Back home, we might be enemies. Here on this boat, we can be friends. But what will we be, once we step on the American shore?"

George thought for a second. "Maybe we can be what we want to be and leave the past behind. They say you can do that here. I'm not sure."

As more passengers began to gather on the deck, the ship dropped its anchor and headed to harbor.

CHAPTER TWO

The first thing George noticed about the city was the steam coming out of the streets. It seemed to come from nowhere, as if the neighborhood had been built above a smoky furnace. The temperature was near boiling, and everything looked hot and sticky, covered with soot and sand. It was different from the gloomy, rainy London weather George had grown up with.

That was not the only shock George experienced as the ship entered the harbor. Americans along the docks moved with an energy that George had never seen, not even in other large cities. Some people walked so fast, they collided with bystanders. And yet they kept moving.

The level of noise surrounding the dock was intense. People everywhere seemed to be screaming at the top of their voices. A peddler was yelling at passersby to try his clothes, insulting them when they refused. A preacher yelled warnings of fire and brimstone at anyone who looked like he might be listening. He passed out Bibles to passengers as they left the boat.

George and Steve Oakley passed the immigration checkpoints together and stepped off the boat. They had no idea which direction they were heading or which neighborhood they were in.

"Let me stop and ask for directions," Steve said, as they walked through a crowded street. Everywhere George looked, there were people: selling things, performing on the street, or begging for change. Steve approached one of the beggars and asked him a question.

"Could you point me to a pub in the Bowery called the Woodrat?"

"Fool! Tourist! The Bowery is clearly to your north!" The beggar pointed wildly in that direction. George then asked the beggar if he could be directed to the New York Times Building. The beggar had no idea what a *New York Times* was. So George continued to follow Steve as he walked north.

The sights and sounds were so disorienting that George failed to notice a young boy, maybe twelve years old, who had walked up behind the two men. He wore clothes similar to the beggar and had a shifty, uncomfortable stare. Suddenly he sprinted forward and grabbed something from Steve's back pocket. Then he ran in the other direction.

"My wallet!" Steve yelled. George turned around, but it was too late. The boy was disappearing in the distance with Steve's wallet in his hand. Without another word, George ran after the boy.

"Wait!" Steve ran after George, who was already far ahead. Not only was George big and strong for his age, but his massive legs gave him incredible running power as well. The boy must have known this, because he only ran so far as a block before he passed the wallet to another beggar, who looked older and much stronger.

The boy had gotten away, but the older man stood at the corner, holding Steve's wallet. George quickly caught up with him and held out his hand.

"My friend's wallet, please," George said. "That boy stole it."

"Kiss off, chum. I didn't see no boy. Belongs to me now." He pushed George's outstretched hand out of the way. George grabbed the man's forearm with his other hand.

"Give it back."

"No."

Without thinking, George clenched his right fist. And with incredible momentum, he punched the beggar in the side of the face. He could feel a tooth cracking against his knuckles as blood spurted from the man's face. The beggar fell over.

A crowd of people in the area began to notice. It surrounded the two men. Steve was among them. They started chanting together. "Fight! Fight! Fight!"

As George grasped his bloody knuckle to lessen the pain, the crowd's chants inspired the beggar to fight back. Dazed, he held his fists up to George's face and began jabbing with all the force he could muster. George was forced to put up his own fists in defense. The beggar rained blows on George's body but never connected a hard punch.

George could see that the beggar was getting tired. He knew his chance would come. For a second, the beggar let down his fists to recover. Just then, George switched from defense to offense and rammed a powerful uppercut into his opponent's jaw. This time, he could hear as well as feel the man's teeth cracking. The uppercut put him down again. The crowd cheered and started chanting louder. "Fight! Fight! Fight!"

The beggar got up for the third time, his mouth and nose still bleeding. George expected to have to defend himself against another few blows. But instead of putting up his fists, the beggar put out his hand, which held Steve Oakley's wallet.

"Thank you," George said and took the

wallet back. As quickly as they had gathered, the circle of fight spectators disappeared. The beggar slinked off. Only Steve remained, happy that he had his wallet back.

"Golly, George!" Steve said. "Are you sure you dinnae want to try your hand at some fights? My brother is looking for men exactly like you."

"No thank you, Steve. I'm still a journalist. Besides, violence bothers me. Did you see how the Americans whooped and cheered as I hurt that man?"

"I did."

"Why didn't they help him?" George asked. "Why did no one try to stop the boy from getting away? And where were the police?"

Steve shrugged. "They say the New York police are just as unsavory as the criminals they put away."

They walked on. Eventually they found someone who was able to give an address for the Times Building: 41 Park Row, right across from city hall. Steve still needed to find his brother on Delancey Street, so the two split up. George promised to visit Steve at the Woodrat soon.

Soon after, George entered the New York Times Building, his fist still throbbing slightly from pain as he clutched the letter from his new employers.

CHAPTER THREE

George had expected to meet with the publisher, Nelson Jones, as soon as he arrived. Instead, he was told to meet with the line editor on the building's fifth floor. George had been anticipating this visit for so long that he bounded up each flight of stairs like an excited child.

He came to the top floor and approached a man sitting at a desk, furiously writing notes on something. The desk was cluttered, and the man's fingers and arms were stained with ink.

He smoked a cigar as he worked. George stood in front of him for what seemed like minutes before the man finally noticed his visitor. There was a name on the desk, also smudged with ink. It read: *V. Thomas*.

"Excuse me, sir . . ." George began gently.

The man barely looked up. "Yes? Mm-hmm?" Then he looked back down.

"George Choogart. Your publisher offered me a job . . ."

"What is that, a British accent?"

George paused. "That is correct. I arrived here from London earlier today."

"George Choogart, George Choogart . . ." The man started trying to recall the name. "Sorry to tell you this, George Choogart, but Nelson Jones, the man who hired you, is dead."

"He is?"

"Of tuberculosis. Happened a few weeks ago. While you were at sea, probably. He was coughing blood. Awful stuff. Kept coming to work. Very distracting."

The man's speaking style was gruff and un-friendly. He was tall and muscular, though not as tall or muscular as George, and was bald except for a few spots of gray hair. Or maybe it was spots of ink. He appeared to be in his early fifties.

George was alarmed. Did this mean that his job was gone? Had he traveled across the Atlantic for nothing?

"Sit down," the man gestured. George sat in a chair across from the desk. "My name is Van Thomas, by the way. Hopefully you never heard of me. I hate it when that happens."

George had not. He reached into his coat pocket and brought out the crumpled, folded letter. "Your paper wrote that my journalism was impressive, and it wanted to hire me."

"Tell me what you did to impress us, because I am very forgetful."

"I exposed a scandal in the House of Lords," George said, "which led to the Tory MP's resignation. Your paper used my information in its reports."

"And how old are you?"

"Eighteen."

"So you were eighteen, and you wrote a story

exposing corruption in the House of Lords?" Van Thomas asked. "How in the world were you allowed access at that level?"

"Just lucky, sir," George said. That was not the full truth.

"Refresh me on this. So the Tory MP was caught serving tainted and poisonous food?"

"To his mistresses, yes. He murdered several women he was carrying on affairs with."

"Those seedy kinds of scandals may sell papers, Mr. Choogart, but that's not what we do at the *Times*. This is the paper that, just last year, blew the whistle on Tammany Hall. Have you Brits heard of Boss Tweed?"

"Certainly."

"Bribery, kickbacks, murder—there is nothing that man would not do to own the city. And we brought him down. With the power of journalism."

"Congratulations," George said.

"Why? The minute we blew the whistle on Tweed, a new fella was put in his place. Have you heard of Big Jim Dickinson?"

"I don't believe so."

"He's like Tweed but worse," Van Thomas said. "A crooked politician who knows how to keep his hands clean. Nelson wanted to hire you because there aren't a lot of reporters ready to stand up to the crooked pols and cops. But you obviously do. Or do you?"

"It is why I am a journalist."

"Still curious, though—who were your sources with the MP? How did a kid like you discover what dozens of Fleet Street vets could not?"

"You know I cannot give away my sources, sir," George repeated. "I am a journalist."

"Good thing too or I would have fired you on the spot. You passed the first test. Now here's the next one. Bring me a story tomorrow. Something about this city that I've never seen or heard of before. If it smells too familiar, you're fired."

How would George know what Van Thomas found familiar? George decided not to ask the question out loud.

"Anything else?" Van Thomas asked. He was ready to get back to work.

There was something else. "I was also told I can expect lodging from the newspaper," George said.

"Ah." Van pulled out a large binder from under his desk and flipped through some pages. "Lucky for you, the *Times* always rents a few extra rooms for the new scribblers. Let me find the address and key."

Van kept searching. "Ah," he finally said. "There's a small apartment on Delancey where you can stay."

"Delancey," George said. "Where have I heard that name?"

Van replied, "It's a big street. Goes right through the Bowery. Have a nice time!"

Before George could ask for a nicer location, he was shooed out of the office with address and key in hand. Van went back to his work, ink smeared across his body like dried black blood.

George left the building and headed north, toward the Bowery—a place he would now call home.

CHAPTER FOUR

George arrived at the row house on Delancey that he was due to call home. Even as a former East Ender, he was surprised at the filthiness of the Bowery. Every nook and cranny of the neighborhood seemed stuffed with grime. Outside the row house, he could hear babies screaming in the heat. Jugglers and poets stood at every corner, begging for money for their services. Flies and mosquitoes hung over everything.

George's lodgings were no cleaner. The row

house was a straight line of rooms, each about the size of a large box. Tenants shared a kitchen at the end of each floor, but it was a mess of disgusting, unwashed dishes. The bathroom wasn't even worth considering.

George sat at a desk table and took off his coat, removing the copy of *Bleak House* and the letter and placing them on the table. As he began to settle in, George heard a knock on the door. George opened it, and a woman stood outside his new place.

She had lengthy, stringy blonde hair that was discolored by the sun. Her clothes were brown and baggy, patched together. Her eyes had a crazed expression, but she seemed friendly.

"New neighbor!" she said, as soon as the door opened. She held a small loaf of bread in her hand and graciously gave it to George.

George held the bread, confused. "Er..."

"Just a little present from a neighbor. Cost me m' day's earnings!"

A richer man might have given the bread back. But George was already used to extreme poverty. He accepted the gift graciously.

The woman walked into the room. "I am Millie. Short for Millicent, but don't call me that, please. Hey, what is that?" She pointed to the book.

"It is a book I brought from home. *Bleak House* by Charles Dickens."

"Wow, a book!" she exclaimed. She opened the book and peaked through the pages. "Thick, at that."

"It is. It's a long book."

"Y' must be a smart fella to read a book like this. You sure you live here?"

"I do, but I'm from England."

Millie took a second to process this. "So that's why your voice is so strange."

George smiled. "Right."

Millie put the book down. "I have to tell my friend Muggs about this. Hey, Muggs!" she shouted down the hall.

A few seconds later, a short man with a long, unruly mustache appeared in the doorway.

"Millie!"

"Muggs! Meet the new neighbor."

George held out his hand for Muggs to

shake. Muggs missed the cue and instead let out a large burp.

"Muggs!" Millie shouted again.

"Sorry, boss," Muggs said, embarrassed.

"So what do you do, Mr. Muggs?" George asked, trying to be polite.

"Call me Muggs. Me an' Millie here run a sort of business."

"We're haberdashers, Muggs," Millie said.

"We're trash scavengers," Muggs retorted. "I got a whole bunch of buttons, ribbons, and scraps of fabric, if you ever need a patching up. Heck, I'll give you a first patch session free of charge!"

"Actually," George said. "I have to leave around now. There's a deadline I need to attend to."

Muggs and Millie stared at George blankly, not entirely sure what a deadline meant.

Suddenly yet another man's voice came from around the corner. "Vagrants! Leave this man's quarters before I call the police again!"

Before George had a chance to understand what was going on, Millie and Muggs had fled the scene. In their place stood a younger, heavy-set man. He was carrying a set of papers.

"Mr. Choogart?"

"Yes," George said.

"I am Mr. Nordler, the landlord. Rent is five dollars per month, to be paid promptly on the first of each month. If you are late, I will not hesitate to call the police."

"Understood."

"Are you a journalist, Mr. Choogart?"

"Yes."

"Lucky for you that I have respect for your vocation. However, you should know that the *Times* has sent journalists to this location before. Not many could handle the lifestyle."

George again recalled his childhood on the East End. "I can."

"We will see. Here are your papers. I want them signed and on my desk within the hour."

Nordler left. George had no time to reflect on the oddness of his neighbors. As he had said, he had a deadline to catch.

———

George spent the next several hours walking around the neighborhood, looking for a story. Now that he had gotten used to the pace of the Bowery, he was starting to like it more. Everywhere he went, there was some form of cheap entertainment. Vaudeville, circus acts, and freak shows. No place ever seemed to close for the evening. In fact, the neighborhood seemed to become even livelier as the sun went down.

George was ready to return home and begin writing when he noticed a big wooden sign outside a large saloon. It read *WOODRAT.* George recalled the name immediately—it was where his new friend Steve Oakley said he had found work.

George made his way toward the doors. Just as he was about to walk in, he heard a loud crash. A man shouted; then a few people shouted with him. Then there was a sound of scuffling and fighting.

George barely had a chance to see what was going on inside before the saloon's heavy door was pushed outward. Two men in a wrestle grip barreled outside. George was right in their way, and he did not have time to move. The men collided with George. The three of them fell into a patch of mud outside the Woodrat, writhing and punching each other.

CHAPTER FIVE

Three men wrestled in a pit of mud outside of the Woodrat. Of the three of them, only George had no idea what was happening or why he was suddenly involved in another fight. The other two were on top of him, still trading blows. George still had enough momentum to push the two men away and scramble to his feet.

The other two men did not seem to even realize George was there. They screamed insults and clutched at each other. The slickness of the mud caused them to lose their grip. They both stood up, fists raised. Without another word, they started circling each other in the muck, waiting for a chance to strike a blow.

Using his mammoth size, George attempted to stand in between the men. "Gentlemen," he pleaded, "what is this about?"

The two men pivoted around him, angry at the interruption.

"Stay out my business," one said. "This man is a cheater!"

The other replied to this plea for peace by socking George in the mouth. The man's enemy did the same to George's stomach. George fell back in the mud. Whatever argument existed between the two brawlers was replaced by a shared urge to gang up on George.

"What are yeh, some sort of limey?" the first man asked, standing over George's prone body.

"This is New York, buddy. No Brit tells us what to do!" said the second man.

George realized that he was likely to die if he did not defend himself. Swiftly, he moved his right leg underneath the first man and tripped him, crashing into the mud. Then he stood up to face the second man.

The second man struck first. He aimed a punch at George's neck, but George was fast enough to block it and grab the man's hand. While the man was unprotected, George struck. First, he aimed a jab to the lower pelvis. Then, as the man doubled over in pain, George sent a chop to the back of his head. Finally, George made the dazed man face him once more. His right fist connected to the man's jaw. There was a cracking sound. The man fell for good. He was out cold.

The first man had freed himself from the mud again. He tried a different strategy, staying an arm's distance away with his fists raised. George did the same. They moved around each other, each waiting for a sign of weakness.

George found a weakness first. The first man moved in and tried to land a kick, but George grabbed the man's foot and delivered a devastating chop to the man's ankles. Then George twisted the foot around as the man howled in pain. From there, all it took was a back-fist blow to the man's head to bring him down.

Two men lay unconscious. George, only a bit scuffed, tried to rub the mud off his clothes. At that moment, another man stepped outside the bar. He was better dressed than the men in the crowd and looked better fed. He did not seem like the type of person who would frequent a grimy bar in the Bowery.

George was prepared for another round of violence, but the man held out his hand instead. "Lew Mayflower," he said. "I own this bar."

"Call me George."

"George, I want to thank you for dealing with this matter, even if it was not intentional."

"What exactly happened between these men?"

"Why don't you come inside?" Mayflower asked. "We can try to clean your clothes, and I would like to reward you for your service. Would you like a drink?"

"No, thanks. But I will take some food."

Lew shouted into his bar. "Give this man a meal!"

George sat at the bar of the Woodrat, eating peas and potatoes from a plate while somebody washed his clothes. It had been a while since he had a satisfying meal. Lew sat with him and named the personnel of the Woodrat.

"That's Tracey," he said, pointing to the bartender serving customers. "My best bartender. He scares customers. That's why I like him. Over there is Silas, a young boy we brought over recently. You could call him a janitor. You could call him a doctor too. The boy knows how to dress a wound."

"Is there a man here named Oakley?" George asked.

Lew frowned. "There was. He's not been present these past two workdays. Not sure why."

"I met his brother, Steve, on my boat ride to America. He said he was looking for work here."

"Oh, Steven," Lew said. "I told him earlier this afternoon that his brother was gone, so Steven went to go find him."

"Find him where? What might have happened?"

Lew put his hand on George's shoulder.

"George, I like you, but it is very important that you keep what I say secret. I trust you. You are an intelligent man who is not afraid of his fists. Even if you are a Brit. Can I trust you?"

"Of course," George said. He decided then to hide the fact that he was a journalist. Nothing shut down a conversation faster than telling a man with secrets that you write for the papers.

"I run fights in this club. Some would call them illegal. Certainly, the police do."

"What does this have to do with Oakley?" George asked.

"Oakley is my enforcer, but he just went missing. You see, recently I've been doing business dealings with Big Jim Dickinson. Big Jim's a major politician in these parts. You may have heard the name."

George did recall the name—Van Thomas had mentioned the man. Big Jim had taken Boss Tweed's spot after Tweed had been thrown in jail.

Lew continued: "Big Jim has been using our club to scout for fighters. See, we put on fights in the Woodrat, but they ain't the main show.

Last few months, Big Jim has been paying me and Oakley to send him our best fighters."

"So what happened?"

"I'm not sure. One day, Oakley said he'd been noticing something suspicious. His guys kept losing at the Big Jim fights. It didn't seem right. So he went to talk to Big Jim. Then he disappeared."

"You think Big Jim did something?"

"I'm sure of it, but keep it under your collar," Lew said. "If Big Jim finds out, he has the power to humiliate us, kill us, throw us in jail . . . whatever he wants."

George realized he might have a story. He needed to go home and write about it.

"Let me ask you a question, George. Are you looking for work?"

George was in too deep now to let anyone know he was employed. "Er . . . no. I've been looking for a job."

"You found one. Come back here tomorrow. I still need fighters, and you clearly have the skills as well as the build. And the money is good. You might like it."

"I accept," George said, though in his mind he hated the idea of inflicting more violence. "But now I have to be leaving."

"Leaving without a single drink, eh? Come back and visit tomorrow evening."

"I will."

As George was about to exit, Lew stopped him and asked another question. "George. What's your last name?"

George tried to summon a name that would keep him from being outed as a journalist. His thoughts turned to *Bleak House*. He remembered a man in Dickens's novel who mysteriously exploded.

"Call me George Krook," he said.

"Krook, eh? I think you'll fit right in at the Woodrat," Lew laughed.

George took the opportunity to leave and walk the several blocks home. When he entered his room, he lit a candle and began to write.

CHAPTER SIX

George returned to the New York Times Building the next day with story in hand. It described the fight he had with the men outside the Woodrat. Then it discussed the mysterious disappearance of the club's fight manager.

Van Thomas read over the article intently, splashing passages with ink at superhuman speed. It took him about a minute to read.

"This is garbage," he said and threw the article out a nearby window.

"What?" George was surprised. He was used to glowing praise from editors.

"You know how many fights in the Bowery happen every day? More than we have space for in the *Times*. This is what we in the business like to call a 'nonstory.'"

"Nonstory?"

"Junk that we've already heard before," Van said. "I told you to come in with a story about something I had never seen, read, or heard about. You failed."

George sat still for a second. "Am I fired? You said I would be fired."

"Believe me, I wish I could fire ya. The sad fact is that we still need a reporter who is incorruptible, who never stops looking for the truth."

"The truth?"

"What I mean is that we need a reporter who isn't on Big Jim's payroll. Someone who hasn't been threatened by his men, someone who's basically unknown in America. So that is you."

"So I get to keep my job," George said.

"You do. But I'm not publishing your junk today."

"What exactly do you want, Mr. Thomas?"

"Look. Fights in bars happen every day. People die every day. Why, just yesterday, at least three different men perished from falling off rooftops. You know why?"

"Why?"

"Because they were sleeping," Van said. "Because the temperature is so hot in some of these poor neighborhoods that families need to sleep outside for relief. So they sleep on the roof. Some of the more restless sleepers roll off the building and die. This happens every summer in the city."

"So you want a story where no one dies."

"How about a story where you say something that no one else has the guts to say? You remember the Tory MP. You took down a powerful man with facts and evidence. You see the sign above the door?"

George read the sign: "The attitude of great poets is to cheer up slaves and horrify despots."

"Walt Whitman said that. *Leaves of Grass*. You understand what that means?" Van asked. "Too many of us go after the poor, the weak, the slaves. Not journalists. Fight the rich and powerful. It is what a journalist should do, always."

"Understood." George said.

"Now leave and try again. Leave out the slaves this time, and find me a despot worth spitting on."

George nodded. Maybe he belonged at the paper more than he thought.

———

Later that night, George returned to the Woodrat. With no other leads to explore, he planned to continue posing as George Krook. Maybe he'd find out what happened to Oakley and his brother. As he walked in through the moving doors, he noticed that only Lew was there. He stood behind the bar, washing out glasses.

"George Krook!" Lew said, upon seeing George. "Come inside."

George moved to the bar. Lew continued cleaning glasses. "I have something of a test for you, before we can move on to other business. Boys?"

From out of the back of the Woodrat, four men appeared. They were all muscular and imposing. They looked ready to hurt something.

"George, I need you to fight these men."

"What?"

"Consider it your first test," Lew said. "Men, I want you to attack George Krook with everything you have. I want him either unconscious or forcibly restrained."

The men charged. Instinctively, George picked up a barstool and flung it at the back of the club. Then he leaped onto the bar.

The men decided to charge him one at a time. The first to try did not even come close. As he approached, George landed a solid roundhouse kick to his face. The man spat blood and hit the ground in less than a second.

Lew, watching with interest, continued cleaning out his glasses.

One of the other men leapt onto the bar, hoping to tackle George face-to-face. The man connected a few blows to George's shoulder and arm, but nothing that caused that much pain. Then he went in for a head punch—a mistake.

In a fraction of a second, George ducked the punch and delivered a blow to the man's rib cage. As the man clutched his chest in pain, George slapped him so hard he fell off the bar to the floor. Two men were now unconscious.

The final two men realized that the mistake had been to attack him one at a time. George took this opportunity to leap off the bar onto a nearby billiards table. He lifted a cue and held it in front of him, to prevent his attackers from getting closer.

Lew said, "Stop."

The attackers backed off and moved away. They collected the two unconscious men and returned to the back room, as if nothing had happened.

"Have Silas dress their wounds," Lew told the others before they disappeared.

"I apologize for the deception, but I needed to see how you fight. Now I know enough."

George gripped the billiards cue so hard his hand ached. He was disgusted by the violence he was responsible for. "What is going on?"

"I told you, Krook—a test. You succeeded.

These men obviously failed. And they were some of my best fighters."

"So you tried to have me beaten to see if I could handle a job."

"It's the Bowery way, boy," Lew said. "The sooner you learn this, the more likely you are to survive."

"So what are you hiring me for?"

"It's not me, son. It's Big Jim Dickinson. With Oakley gone, I've stepped in as temporary recruiter. And Big Jim needs you. Do you accept?"

George thought of his earlier conversation with Van Thomas. Cheer slaves and anger despots. From what he knew, Big Jim Dickinson was a despot worth targeting.

"I accept."

"Good, Mr. Krook. Be here tomorrow, and I'll introduce you to Big Jim."

George Choogart finally had a lead on something big.

<hr>

George met with Van Thomas the next morning with nothing to show the editor.

"Are you trying to get yourself fired?" Thomas asked.

"I have a lead, Mr. Thomas, but it requires follow-up."

"A lead?" Van barked. "What kind of lead?"

"I would prefer to not share that information."

"Wow, you really aim to please your editors," Van said. "Give me a hint."

George considered what to say. "It involves Big Jim Dickinson."

Van's face lit up. "If you have something on Big Jim, I need to know."

"Not yet. Let me gather some more information tonight."

"All right. Listen, George, you need to be careful around Big Jim. I've had several reporters watch him who came back dead. He owns the police; he owns city hall. He can't be touched without a whole lot of proof that he is involved in illegal activities. Right now, I have a reporter on the inside of Big Jim's operation, but she needs to maintain her cover."

She? George thought.

"George, never let anyone know you are a

journalist. And be careful. I can't have you die before you deliver a big scoop, after all."

"Thanks for your kind concern, sir."

"You're welcome. Now get out of my office and come back with something interesting, for once."

That evening, George returned to the Woodrat. Lew, Silas, and Tracey were all there, as were a collection of regular customers. As soon as George entered, Lew rushed him into a back room.

"George, you're about to be my next great fighter. Big Jim wants the best that I have, and that seems to be you."

"Will I fight tonight?"

"Not tonight," Lew said. "Tonight I show you where Big Jim holds his bouts. You have to swear to me you will never tell another man about the location."

"I swear," George said. He felt guilty, not letting on that he was a journalist. But there was no way that Lew would let him attend if Lew knew that.

Lew barked some instructions to his employees. Then he and George hit the Bowery streets. They passed amateur theaters, concert halls, and flophouses before coming upon a curiously clean, large house. There were two guards in front of the entrance.

"Stay here," Lew said. He went to talk to the guards. After a short conversation, Lew called to George. "Come on in, Krook."

George entered the house. It was the opposite of everything else he had seen in the Bowery. Chandeliers larger than human beings hung from high ceilings. The furniture looked new, as if it had never been touched.

"This is . . . very nice," George said, trying to think of a better word.

"It pays to be rich. But we go downstairs." Lew pointed to a staircase that led underground.

As they walked down the long staircase, George began to hear noises. First, they were faint. Then he could hear loud cheering.

"We're getting closer," Lew said.

The bottom of the staircase led to a room that seemed to have an even higher ceiling than the main floor. It was massive.

In the center of the room, George saw a large ring with two men inside. Cheering, shrieking spectators surrounded the ring. But these were not the people that George expected. The men in the audience wore three-piece suits and hats. The women all wore gowns and fancy jewelry. The only poorly dressed people were the men in the ring—and George, who still wore his single pair of clothes.

"This is where the rich folk come to place their bets," Lew whispered to George, as an usher led them to their seats. "Not what you expect from the Bowery streets, eh?"

"I've never seen anything like it," George said. The size of the ring, the noise, and the spectacle were intense.

"Every major politician, every donor to the Tammany cause, every crooked cop is here tonight. Along with their wives. Let me tell you, the women here are no more innocent than the men."

An announcer walked into the center of the ring, and the crowd started to quiet down.

"Ladies! Gentlemen! Please welcome . . . the honorable Big Jim Dickinson!"

The crowd roared as Big Jim entered from a side room and made his way through the crowd. It was easy to see why he was called Big Jim. Put politely, he was a heavyset person. A body man trailed behind him, ready to support him in case he started falling. Slowly and with much difficulty, Big Jim traveled across the room to sit in his special seat, in front of all the other spectators, right outside the ring.

Big Jim spoke: "We have two fighters today of considerable power. The first is my man, Al Stevens."

Al Stevens, the bigger man, held up his hand in recognition. He was massive, larger than George. His face looked bent and broken from years of taking punches.

"In the other corner," Big Jim continued, "his opponent, Ed 'Steam Train' Johnson!"

The man they called Steam Train lifted his fists in the air as the crowd screamed. He was shorter and less muscular than Al Stevens but perhaps twice as ugly.

"Folks, I know your time and money is precious, and I have no intention of wasting either. Begin the fight!"

The fight began at Big Jim's request. Steam Train and Al moved toward each other with fists raised over their face, waiting for the other to make the first move. They jabbed at each other a few times, not really connecting.

Then Al Stevens decided to move in for the kill. He lunged toward his opponent and tried to lock his arms around the other man's neck. This left Steam Train an opening to land a few small blows. One connected with his stomach, while the other grazed Stevens's lower neck and chin. Stevens fell back, dazed.

Lew leaned over to explain to George. "Al Stevens is a big man but not too smart. Fighting's as much about brains as it is about strength. Look at the way Steam Train dodges and moves."

Indeed, even though Steam Train was smaller, he seemed to be winning. Quickness and agility seemed to be the best solution against a fighter like Al.

Steam Train kept winning. Al couldn't land a punch no matter how hard he hurled it. He was looking tired.

George noticed Big Jim's face as he looked on the fight intently. He was visibly angry. Clearly, he had betted on Al Stevens.

Though victory for Steam Train seemed assured, he suddenly looked over to Big Jim and froze in his tracks. He only paused for a second, but that gave Al time to recover. Without hesitation, Al rained a series of blows on Steam Train's head. Steam Train fell to the ground, twitching. The fight was over, but Al began angrily stomping on Steam Train's chest. He leaned over the dazed fighter, brought his fist in the air, and brought it down on Steam Train's face. Then he did it again.

"He's going to kill him!" George whispered in Lew's ear.

"If that's what it takes for Big Jim to make his winnings, then that's what will happen. Like I said, it's the Bowery way."

George and Lew both left the house after the match.

"What did you think, Krook?" Lew asked as they walked over the neighborhood streets and cobblestones."

George had never been so disgusted and so curious at the same time.

"Lew, the other man, Steam Train, seemed to be winning. What happened?"

Lew paused. "I'm not sure. But it seems like Big Jim's man always wins, and he always gets the money. How about that?"

Something smelled like a story.

"George, I want to set a match with you tomorrow. Do you agree?"

"I do. Who with?"

"Al Stevens."

George wanted to protest, but he knew he had to face Al Stevens if he ever wanted to get closer to Big Jim. He barely slept that night, restless at the idea of what might happen in the ring the next day.

CHAPTER SEVEN

The next morning, when George arrived in Van Johnson's office, someone else was seated in the chair across from the editor's desk. It was the woman that Van had briefly mentioned earlier.

A female reporter, George thought. He had heard of such a thing but rarely seen it. Certainly in England, a woman was expected to be seen and not heard, the opposite of what was expected from a newspaperman. Journalism was thought to be a man's profession. George assumed this was just as true in the States.

Van looked up from his desk, where he and the woman were going over some writing. "George, you have an article for me today?"

"Not today, Van."

"George, you've turned wasting my time into an art. I want you to meet Holly Quine, our 'stunt' reporter.'"

"What does that mean?" George asked.

"It means a woman can't be a successful journalist unless given a silly name, Mr. Choogart," Holly said.

Van spoke: "I wanted to introduce you to Holly so you can compare notes on Big Jim Dickinson. You are still looking at the Dickinson story, right?"

"Not only that," George replied, "but I'm feeling out a major scoop."

"Tell me no more, George. I'm going to step out for some breakfast. Feel free to continue to talk to Holly. Or don't—I definitely do not care."

The editor stepped out of the building. George and Holly were alone. Holly had a serious face and a small nose. George could tell, from her expression alone, how sharp she was.

"Mr. Choogart, for the last several months I have been running undercover operations for the *Times*. I assume you've heard of the Tweed scandal?"

"Boss Tweed?" George said. "I heard he purloined millions of dollars from city citizens."

"Try billions, Mr. Choogart. I helped bring the *Times* the information that brought Tweed down last year."

"Congratulations," George said. "That's quite an accomplishment."

"For a woman, you mean? Don't bother with your half-compliments, Mr. Choogart. I'm a better journalist than anyone in this building, including you."

"Sorry."

"Apologies are also unnecessary," Holly said. "My point is that Tweed was locked up, but the system that allowed Tammany Hall to rob us is still in place. My belief is that Big Jim Dickinson is the new ringleader, but I've yet to find proof."

"How do you know?"

"I am allowed access to certain places that male journalists are not. I can pretend to be a moronic, man-obsessed society woman, and in return the men of Tammany Hall provide me favors and information. When they least expect it, of course."

"But you still have nothing solid against Dickinson."

"Not yet," Holly said. "He is more secretive than Tweed, less prone to parading his wealth for everyone to see. Make no mistake—he gorges on fancy duck, pork tenderloin, all the finest foods, while the rest of us starve. The difference is he doesn't eat in public."

"I understand. So you need my help."

"Have you found anything?" Holly asked.

"Yes. But I would prefer to keep it to myself for now. It's my story, after all."

Holly Quine frowned and then spoke very slowly. "Mr. Choogart. Maybe it was different for you in London, but here at the *Times*, we actually aspire to convey the news, not just hog our own slice of glory."

George reasoned for a second. "Holly, I will make a deal with you. I have a meeting tonight where I might have access to Big Jim. Let me find out more before I break the information. According to your editor, Big Jim has killed a few reporters who got too close."

"We can't prove the deaths, of course," Holly said. "All made to look like suicides. Remember, Dickinson owns the police. The only way to stop a man like him is to expose him, very, very publicly."

"Give me tonight to find out more. Then I will share my information. But be careful, Holly." ·

"I certainly didn't get this far by being careful, Mr. Choogart. And I'm not about to start."

———

George returned to his small room later that day to prepare for the night's bout. Lew had given him some fighting clothes to wear, so not to spoil his one garment. As he was putting his clothes on, there was a knock at the door.

"Who is it?" George asked.

"Millie!" a voice shouted.

"Muggs!" another voice shouted.

George opened the door. Millie and Muggs bounded in.

"Good evening, Mr. Choogart," Millie spoke first, as Muggs sniffed around the room. "Any need for a haberdasher today?"

"Not today, Millie. Ask me tomorrow. These clothes might get a bit more worn."

Muggs spoke up. "The landlord says you are a journalist."

George was alarmed. It was not in anyone's best interest to know that he was a journalist, now that he was so deep undercover. "Millie, Muggs—I need to ask a favor of you both," he said.

"Buttons, tunics, scraps of cloth. What're you needing?" Muggs replied.

"None of that. I need you to keep quiet about my being a journalist."

"Why?" Millie asked.

"I can't explain. But it is important you say nothing about me to anyone. You do that, and I promise I have work for you tomorrow."

"Of a haberdashery sort?"

"Of that exact sort," George said.

"Muggs," Millie said to her friend. "We have a real, actual customer!" They were both so excited that they quickly fled the room.

Glad that the conversation ended, George left for Big Jim's secret house.

———————

George met Lew Mayflower outside Big Jim's estate. Lew was about to lead George in again, when George stopped him.

"Lew, I want a favor."

Lew grinned. "Spoken like an American."

"Can I meet Big Jim?"

Lew paused, thinking. "I'll see what I can do."

They passed the guards, entered the house, and went downstairs. The crowd that evening was bigger than the previous night. George went to sit down, while Lew went into the back room where Big Jim was waiting. Not long after, Lew came out and sat next to George.

Lew leaned over. "Big Jim doesn't want to meet you. He's very secretive, you understand."

"I do."

"But I made a deal," Lew said. "Big Jim promises five minutes of his time, on one condition: that you win tonight's fight."

"With Al Stevens?" George said.

"That's right."

George was suddenly very, very concerned. His undercover operation now depended on his skills in the ring. This was going to be a tougher fight than George had thought.

CHAPTER EIGHT

Lew and George moved to opposite corners of the ring. Al Stevens wrapped his knuckles in bandages, rubbing his fists together and waiting for the fight to start.

"You're a big man, Krook," Lew said, "but Al Stevens could dwarf a giant. No one could take more than a few blows."

"What do I do?" George considered breaking his cover and running for an exit.

"The trick is to keep moving and keep him

angry. Stevens is a mountain, but he's slow. As long as you dodge his blows, you have the advantage."

The announcer entered the ring to introduce Big Jim. As the crowd of rich, connected New Yorkers cheered and clapped, Big Jim move to his reserved seat and began to speak.

"Ladies and gentlemen! We welcome our new contender, arrived freshly from the Woodrat. George Krook!"

The crowd cheered George, but not very much.

"In the other corner, we see last night's winner—Al Stevens!"

Much more cheering.

"Begin the bout!"

Al Stevens lunged toward his opponent. George felt a surge of adrenaline, and he dodged Al's first attack. This did not make Al Stevens happy.

The crowd screamed Stevens's name as the two men circled each other. Big Jim sat in silence. George looked out into the crowd, but Lew was nowhere to be found.

Lew's strategy seemed to work. Every time Al got close, George would duck and weave, then land a few punches in the bigger man's torso. Al was so big and so slow that it was easy to move around or under him. The more that George connected, the slower Al got.

Al was angry and huffing. He used the full force of his body to lunge at George. George moved out of the way, but Al's momentum was such that the big man hit the ground, face-first.

Quickly, George locked Al's hands behind his back and started delivering sharp punches to the back of his head. A few of these and Al would lose consciousness. Al could not move, but he yelled strange curses as he lay trapped under George.

The audience was visibly shocked by the reversal of fortunes. A sharp voice pierced the screams of the crowd. "Stop!" It was the voice of Big Jim Dickinson.

The crowd quieted. George took his weight off Al's body. He offered his hand to help Al stand up, but Al wasn't the type of fighter to accept anyone's help.

Big Jim spoke. "Ladies and gentlemen, it is with utmost sadness that I declare a draw for tonight. Unfortunately, political matters demand my immediate attention. Please leave. And Al, return to your quarters."

Al gathered himself up and glared at George, who silently prepared for the larger man's retaliation.

Big Jim stood up with a great deal of effort and faced his audience. "I submit we postpone this event for two days from now. All bettings for tonight are mooted; please see my bookie to place your new bets. Good night!"

The confused audience slowly left the room. Al Stevens sulked and left as well. Soon the only people in the large, empty auditorium were George, Big Jim, and Big Jim's body man.

"You earned your five minutes with me, young man," Big Jim said. "Tell me what you want."

George wrapped some rags around his bloodied fists. "Where did Lew go?"

"Lew Mayflower? I am sorry to say, he is no longer welcome in this club."

"Why?"

"As you can guess, Krook, I run a business that requires secrecy and loyalty from all my transactors. Lew was asking questions, something about one of his employees."

Oakley, George thought.

"Forget Mayflower, boy. You work for me now. I'm told you moved here from the other side of the Atlantic. What brings a Brit like you to the Bowery?"

George lied to maintain cover. "I was charged with a murder. Beat a man to death with my fists for talking to my wife. I fled the country and arrived here. Now I need work."

"I appreciate a man who is . . . flexible with the law. Are you willing to continue your fight with Al Stevens, two nights from now?"

"Sir," George began to explain, "I barely survived this one bout."

"Don't worry, boy. I say your chances of winning are . . . very likely."

"How would you know that?"

"Just trust me," Big Jim said. "I canceled your first fight prematurely for a reason, after all. Oh, it looks like five minutes have passed. Good night, Mr. Krook. See you soon."

With his body man holding up his large frame, Big Jim escorted George from the house. George walked home that night, his mind buzzing with fresh journalism.

———————

George arrived at the *Times* office the next day, a freshly written article in his hands. When he got to Van Thomas's office, however, he received a rude shock. Before anything was said, Van handed him the morning's newspaper.

"Read." Van said. Then he turned to his work.

George scanned the article. *UNDER-GROUND FIGHT RING HAS SECRET TAMMANY CONNECTIONS*, it read. Then George ran the byline: *BY HOLLY QUINE.*

"How did Holly find this?" George asked.

"By following you, Mr. Choogart," Holly said, appearing from around the corner of Van's office.

"You did what?"

"Like I said, I'm a professional journalist," Holly replied. "This means I possess certain skills, such as following and evading detection."

"I told you to give me a day to tell you what I know," George said.

"A good story never waits. And besides, you are posing undercover, correct? Putting your name on this byline would only expose you. It would not take a man with Big Jim's resources much time to connect George Choogart to George Krook."

Though angry at being scooped, George realized Holly was right.

"George, it won't take long until Big Jim starts looking for me," Holly said. "And I mentioned an anonymous source in the article. Big Jim will be searching for a leak among his own people."

"I can't hide now," George said. "I don't think this fight ring is the whole story."

"How is that?"

George was about to explain how his friend, Lew Mayflower, had disappeared during the fight. How he had questioned Big Jim about the

Oakley brothers' disappearance just before that. Then he caught himself. Holly was already in trouble with Big Jim, and that knowledge could harm her.

"The story is mine, Holly," George said.

"Don't insult me, Mr. Choogart," Holly snapped. "Underneath your tall, muscular physique, you abhor violence, don't you? You'd better hurry, before Big Jim finds out you prefer writing to fighting."

Van suddenly spoke up. "This conversation is ruining my day. Just as you, George, have ruined most of my week. I no longer have the words to adequately express how close you are to being fired."

"Give me two more days, Mr. Thomas."

"What do you think, Ms. Quine?" The editor turned to Holly.

"If he needs the extra time, give it to him. I have my own sources. We will talk again soon, Mr. Choogart."

George knew now for certain: if he didn't have a story by the following night, he was finished in this city.

CHAPTER NINE

George Choogart was finally beginning to understand the Bowery streets. As he walked from the Times Building back home, he was no longer shocked by the levels of noise or steam or commotion on the busy streets. He was getting used to it all. Maybe, George thought, New York could still be a home for him.

Of course, that would not matter if George did not have a story that nailed Big Jim. Everything depended on the rematch with Al Stevens, set for the night that followed. In the meantime, George had to follow some of his leads.

First, he walked to the Woodrat. It was the middle of the day, and the establishment was locked and closed down. George attempted to look through a small window, but no one was outside. Then he noticed a young man outside the club, absently sweeping the streets. It took him a second, but George remembered the boy. It was Silas, the janitor.

"Silas? Do you remember me? I'm George Krook."

Silas looked up from the cobblestones he was sweeping. "Of course I remember you, Mr. Krook. Mr. Mayflower spoke much of you in the last few days."

"Silas, where is Lew?"

Silas shrugged. "I never seen the club closed, no matter what time of day. I woke up and walked to work, just like I always do. The Woodrat was locked. So, I figure I stay here and sweep the walkway until Mr. Mayflower returns."

George did not have the heart to tell Silas that Mayflower was not likely to return.

"Silas, maybe you should go home. Mr. Mayflower is taking a day off from work."

"Sir, Mr. Mayflower never takes the day off. I will wait until he returns."

So George left Silas outside the Woodrat, still sweeping. It was now clear that Lew had been taken, and his captor was Big Jim Dickinson. Could the same thing happen to Holly Quine?

George needed to find out. But first he decided to go home.

_____

A rude shock awaited George as soon as he stepped into his room. His few belongings— a table, a bed, and some papers—were overturned, destroyed, or ripped to bits. It seemed as though someone had searched George's room inside and out. Before George had a chance to determine what happened, there was a knock on the door.

"Who is it?" George asked.

"Muggs!" said one voice.

"Millie!" said another.

"This is your landlord, George," said a third voice. "I'm here with Muggs and Millie."

George opened the door and let the three inside.

"There were men who came to search your room, George," Muggs said.

"For what?"

"They didn't say, but they were very pushy," Millie said. "Kept asking us questions. But we did what you told us."

"What was that?" George had forgotten.

"They asked everyone in the hall what we knew about you. What you did for a living," Muggs said. "We said we didn't know."

George understood. "So you did not tell anyone I was a journalist?"

"And sell out my favorite customer? Not a chance, sir," Millie said.

Nordler spoke. "Mr. Choogart, I want an explanation. Those men were no mere gangsters or thieves. Are you hiding from someone?"

"I promise I will explain, Mr. Nordler. For now, it is important that no one is aware I am a journalist."

Nordler prodded for more. "What exactly are you planning, Mr. Choogart?"

George was not sure, but he knew his next step was to find Holly. He looked at his desk and noticed something was missing.

"Millie, have you seen my copy of *Bleak House*?"

"Your copy of what?"

"The book I had. Where did it go?"

"Wasn't me, sir. I ain't no thief but a professional haberdasher. Completely different."

"I have to leave," George said. He brushed past a confused Muggs, Millie, and Mr. Nordler, and made his way back outside to the Bowery streets.

———————

George's next stop was back to the *Times* office, to see if Holly was still there. Unfortunately, Holly and Van were both out of the building. That by itself was not a good sign.

George realized he had no choice: he had to go visit Big Jim Dickinson. But Big Jim wasn't expecting him until the next day. George needed an excuse for dropping by. He had to learn what happened to Holly Quine, at any cost. Even if it meant breaking his cover and endangering his own life.

CHAPTER TEN

The soles of George's shoes were completely worn by a few days' walking. He journeyed through the Bowery all day, looking for any clue that might help him find Holly Quine or Lew Mayflower. The *Times* office was still empty, as was the Woodrat. George had one place left to look: the home of Big Jim Dickinson.

Two guards were posted in front. Neither of them would allow George passage.

"I work for Big Jim. I need to see him,"

George told the guards.

"A limey foreigner like yourself looking for Big Jim? You must mistake us for fools."

"It is the truth, sir," George said. "I come with an urgent message. Can you let him know I am present?"

The two guards looked at each other. One of them spoke. "All right. I will let Jim know that . . ."

"George Krook," George said.

". . . George Krook is here."

"Thank you."

The first guard now whispered to the second. "Grab him."

"What?" George tried to ask. The second guard forced back George's arms and put a pair of cuffs around his wrist.

"Like I said, I'll go talk to Big Jim Dickinson," the first guard sneered. "If he says he never heard of you . . . well . . ."

"The cuffs won't come off," the second guard said. "Least not as long as you're alive. Which won't be for very long, if Big Jim don't know the name Krook."

The first guard went inside, while the second guard watched George. If George was caught, he had nowhere to run to.

After a few agonizing minutes, the first guard opened the door and beckoned to the second guard. They exchanged whispers and then turned to George.

"Come on in, son. Big Jim is expecting you."

They removed George's cuffs and led him inside, slamming the door behind him. George still sensed trouble. He moved slowly through a long hall, toward the main living room. The door that led to the basement staircase was closed from view.

Inside the living room, Big Jim was reclining on a long leather couch. "Come in and sit down, Mr. Krook," he said. "Or should I call you Mr. Choogart?"

George froze. He did not sit down.

"My men followed you home last night, George. They had a few conversations with your neighbors. Care to explain?"

George had to think fast. "It's like I told you," he said. "I murdered a man in my home country. To escape, I needed to change my name and hide fast. So I called myself Krook."

"The exploding man from *Bleak House*, right?" Big Jim held up the book that had been stolen from George's room earlier in the day. "Here, have it back," he said.

George took his book back and gripped its pages in his hands.

"I may not look it, Mr. Choogart, but I am a cultured man. I know my Dickens. You would have been wise not to deceive me. I do not like being deceived. In fact, those who try rarely stay alive."

"I swear, Big Jim, I am who I say I am."

"If that is so, why do I hear your neighbors were so unwilling to name your occupation? What is it you do, Mr. Choogart?"

"Whatever you want me to do," George lied.

Big Jim smiled. "Loyalty. Such a lovely human tendency. Sometimes I visit Tweed in prison and ask him for advice. You know what he says about loyalty?"

"What's that?" George asked.

"Anyone can fake it."

"Let me prove my worth to you, Big Jim. Please." George was no longer sure if he was pleading to maintain his cover or pleading for his life.

"Lucky for you that I do have a task," Big Jim said. "It is interesting that you came here when you did. Do you know Holly Quine?"

"No," George said, trying to sound like he was telling the truth.

"She writes for the *New York Times*. Have Tweed tell you about her sometime."

"What do you want with her?"

"This morning, the *Times* printed a story accusing me of running underground fights."

"But you do," George said.

"Yes. And by themselves, the reported rumors of a woman scribbler are not enough to mean anything. But this woman has been following me for weeks. She knows about . . . other operations."

George knew what was coming next.

"I want you to find Ms. Quine, kill her, and throw her corpse in the East River." Big Jim said this flatly, as if he were ordering breakfast.

George suppressed his fear. "How do I find her?"

"I suggest you use violence and intimidation, Mr. Choogart. They've always worked for me. The office of the *New York Times* might be a start."

"Fine," George said. "Am I still scheduled for tomorrow's fight?"

"You are, Mr. Choogart, but this is your first priority. I would not worry about preparing for tomorrow's fight."

"With Al Stevens?" George said. "How can I not be prepared?"

"Leave it alone, Mr. Choogart. As I said, I am confident you will win."

"What do you mean?"

"What I mean is what I say I mean," Big Jim said. "Now, please, deal with Ms. Quine. I will be waiting here for confirmation of her death."

George left Big Jim's house knowing he had to do what the big man said. He had to go back to the New York Times Building.

———

When he returned to his place of work, George found Van Thomas at his usual desk.

"Van, I need to see Holly Quine now."

Van looked up from his work. "Not happening. Holly is in danger. I've placed her in a safe house that only I know about."

"I know Ms. Quine is in danger," George said, "and I think I know what Big Jim is hiding."

"What is that?"

"Tomorrow, I'm supposed to fight a man who has no compunctions about beating me to death. But Big Jim seems confident that I will win."

"You went to talk to Big Jim?" Van asked.

"Yes."

"What did he say?"

"He told me to find and kill Holly Quine."

Silence hung in the air.

"And you want to find her, eh?" Van said. "Listen, George. You already know that a good journalist protects his sources. And a good editor protects his journalists."

"Van, please. Give me her location, or I will have to find it some other way."

"How do you plan to do that?"

"With my fists, if necessary."

Van Thomas sat back in his chair. "I will do anything to protect the location of Holly Quine. You sure you want to start something?"

George had no choice. *So be it*, he thought.

CHAPTER ELEVEN

The editor and his reporter stood motionless, each man waiting for the other to move. George spoke first: "Van, perhaps I am not explaining myself. Big Jim wants my opponent to throw the fight. That way, when I win, he keeps all the money from bets placed against me. This whole operation was designed to take money from people who do not know the bout is rigged."

"A good editor demands proof," Van said. "Where's your proof?"

"I have none, other than the word of Big Jim. That's why I need Holly Quine."

"I will let Holly know you called, but dangerous people are after her. Her location will remain classified."

"Give me her location, Van!" George had reached the end of his patience. He grabbed his editor's desk and flipped it over with a loud crash. Van's papers and items scattered to the floor.

The editor was surprisingly calm. "Choogart, you are this close to feeling my boot in your face. Back away and go home."

George couldn't. He leapt over the overturned desk and grabbed Van by the collar. "Give me the address!" he yelled.

Van gasped out his words as George held his shirt. "You can't ... push ... this editor around." Then he stuck two ink-stained thumbs in George's eye sockets.

George lessened his grip, which gave Van the space to wrap his own arms around George's torso. The editor body-slammed George into the hard floor.

As the two men scrambled and grabbed at each other, Van tried to jab at George's face. George was too quick, however, and his large fist caught Van's. Using that momentum, George forced Van off the ground and rolled out of his way.

Both men stood up, already exhausted and breathing heavily. George tried to reason with the older man. "Van, please stop. We can go to see Holly together. But I need her information before tomorrow night."

"Holly doesn't need your help, George. She's one of our best journalists. You're a limey who can't make a deadline. And I'm about to demonstrate why they call me a two-fisted editor."

"You're trying to bait me, Van. One last chance. I just want Holly's address. For her protection."

"Come and get it, boy."

George leapt over the desk with his right foot extended. His heel connected with Van's cheek. Blood exploded out of the side of the man's face. Van stood recovering from the blow with his hands over his mouth. Blood mixed with the black ink stained on his hands.

George had the advantage. He leveled a ferocious punch into the man's rib cage. A second later, he landed another punch at neck level. Van doubled over in pain. George exerted all the pressure he could on Van's back, which brought him tumbling face-first to the floor.

Van didn't make a sound after that. He was out.

George searched furiously through Van's collections of papers, which were strewn all about the floor. He found bits and pieces of articles, but no other information. Then he noticed a small brown folder on the floor labeled *SAFE HOUSES*.

George opened the folder. There was one address. George removed the sheet with the information he needed and left the Times Building. His boss was still prone on the floor, unconscious. If there was ever a way George could explain this, he needed to start thinking now.

Just before he left the room, George's eyes had returned to the Whitman quote that Van carried above his desk.

"The attitude of great poets is to cheer up slaves and horrify despots."

Hopefully, someday, Van would understand. Sometimes, horrible acts were required to stand up against the worst despots.

———

George scoured the city until he found Holly's safe house. It was a small room in a flophouse not that different from George's. He entered silently and walked to the room specified in Van's folder. He knocked on the door, and for a long while, no one came.

"Holly!" George yelled outside the room. "It's me, George!"

Holly opened the door just a crack. "How did you find me here? Did Van Thomas send you?"

"Sort of," George said. Now was probably not the time to tell her about the bloody duel between reporter and editor.

"Mr. Choogart, you've officially placed me and the rest of the *Times* organization in danger. Did you know Big Jim's men searched my house?"

"They did the same to me. Look, Holly, I think I know the secret behind Big Jim's underground fights."

"You mean, how Big Jim is hustling his Tammany friends by staging fights and having the most likely loser win? You mean he's paying his fighters to throw the fight, so Big Jim can collect money from the bets?"

George was astonished. "How did you know?"

"By checking the financial records of some of Big Jim's friends. Mr. Choogart, this is very different from the Tweed operation. Tweed was stealing from the poor and giving to his friends. Big Jim is stealing from his friends and giving to himself."

"Which means that once we expose him, all his friends will turn on him," George said.

"That is very likely, Mr. Choogart. I assume you took this information from Big Jim himself?"

"Holly, I've been pretending to work for Big Jim in order to get closer, but now I'm scheduled in a fight against Al Stevens that I can't lose."

"Then you must find a way to lose."

"Lose against Al Stevens?" George said. "He will beat me to death afterward."

"Not if Big Jim is forcing him to throw the fight. He will pretend to fight hard, but in the end, his goal is to go down, to make money for Big Jim. If you thwart him, you thwart Big Jim, and the house of cards comes down."

"Holly, there's more. A man named Lew Mayflower also suspected that his fighters were being used. He helped me, and then he disappeared. Can you help me find him?"

"If he's alive, I will need to check local prison or asylum records."

"Do it. I have a fight to prepare for."

George turned to leave.

"Good luck, Mr. Choogart," Holly said. "Or should I say 'bad luck'? In any case, try not to win."

Easier said than done.

———

George spent the next day training for the fight. He was motivated by words Lew Mayflower had given him earlier: "The trick is to keep moving and keep him angry. Stevens is a mountain, but he's slow. As long as you dodge his blows, you have the advantage."

The problem was George did not want the advantage. He needed to lose the bout without arousing suspicion or being beaten to death by Al Stevens. As George practiced his jabs, hooks, and uppercuts, one question was on his mind: *How can I win by losing?*

The event arrived before George could figure out the answer. George returned to Big Jim's house, where spectators were already starting to gather. He went down the long flight of stairs and entered Big Jim's office. Big Jim was in the middle of a conversation with Al Stevens.

"Remember, Al, I want you to play hard for the first few minutes, but then you need to go down," Big Jim said.

"But . . . but, Big Jim, sir! This man humiliated me! He almost beat me! There's no way I can let that go."

"Exactly why I've bet all my earnings on Krook, Al. Everybody in this audience expects you to seek revenge. In fact, I suspect many are looking forward to watching you beating him to death."

"I know I am," Al said.

"Maybe tomorrow. But not tonight."

Both Big Jim and Al noticed George, standing in the doorway.

"Mr. Krook!" Big Jim exclaimed, gesturing for him to come into the office. "I hope you don't mind me calling you Krook instead of Choogart."

"Of course not, Big Jim."

Al glared at his opponent and then turned to Big Jim. "Can't believe I'm throwing a fight to this fool!"

"Quiet, Al. George, are you ready to perform?"

"Yes, sir."

"Then let's not waste any more time," Big Jim said. "The people want to see a show, after all."

The fight was about to begin. George and Al stood in their corners. Al glared at George with what were clearly murderous intentions. George was scared but tried not to show it.

Big Jim addressed the crowd: "Ladies and gentlemen. I would like to thank you for allowing me to postpone our previous fight. However, I always aim to please my audience, so I am proud to present Al Stevens vs. George Krook, redux!"

The crowd cheered. "Get 'im again, Al!" someone roared. Others shouted in approval. Not a lot of people seemed to be rooting for Krook. Clearly, most of the wealthy onlookers had placed their bets on the bigger man, just like Big Jim wanted.

"Begin the bout!" Big Jim shouted.

The crowd roared even louder, and the fight began.

George and Al Stevens approached each other from their corners. Al still had a vengeful, angry look on his face. It was taking all his self-control to keep from rushing George and beating him to death.

George recalled Lew Mayflower's words one more time: "Keep moving; keep him angry." He put up his fists in a defensive gesture.

Al was the first man to strike. He moved in and chopped at George's shoulder. It connected. George's upper body exploded with pain. It felt like a tap from a wrecking ball.

The crowd cried with pleasure at this first attack. Al moved in for another hit. Then, perhaps remembering Big Jim's warnings, he backed off.

George kept his arms up and debated his next strategy. Al threw another punch, slow on purpose. George ducked and moved sideways. Then he aimed both fists into Al's solar plexus. There wasn't much power to his punch, but Al pretended to be in pain. George couldn't tell anymore if his opponent was fighting to win or fighting to lose.

Al wasn't much of an actor. The crowd almost couldn't believe a big man like Stevens would double over so easily. His cry of "Ow!" was not convincing. Instead of cheering, people in the crowd began to murmur.

George knew now that his best chance was to make Al look as though he was deliberately losing the fight. Since Al could not throw any hard punches, George would not throw any, either.

The fighters circled each other for seconds, then a minute, then two minutes. Neither of them struck a blow. Al's eyes were confused, as if asking, "Why don't you come at me?"

The crowd soon became bored. People started to boo.

"C'mon, Al! Stop pussyfooting about!"

"Pound this fool senseless, Stevens!"

Al looked helplessly to Big Jim, as if he'd missed out on some secret instructions. Big Jim did not return the man's gaze. Al was on his own. So was George.

George could see that Al was becoming angrier as the crowd continued to bait him. This gave him another idea. He began to join the audience in heckling the bigger fighter.

"C'mon, Al!" George said with a crafty grin, circling his opponent. "Why don't you fight back?"

"Yeah!" someone else in the crowd said. "What's going on here?"

George noticed Big Jim getting nervous. The man's eyes darted back and forth.

"Did I hurt you too bad before?" George said. "Are you too scared to get up close?"

Al suddenly became very still. "What did you say?"

"Oh, nothing," George replied. "Except you're a coward."

As if a switch went on in his head, Al had had enough.

"Come here, you maggot." Al Stevens lunged forward.

George knew that now was the time to put his agility to use. Al began to toss deadly punches at the other fighter, punches that could knock a normal man flat. He aimed for George's head, but George ducked. Al tried to get in closer and grab hold of George, but George slithered out of his grip. Al tried to swipe George's legs out from beneath him, but George jumped out of danger. By this time, the audience was puzzled by the lack of action. And Big Jim did not appear to be happy, either.

"Try to touch me, you tosser," George said.

Al responded with a series of curse words, many of which George did not recognize.

The fight continued in this manner. Al threw punches with all his might, and George dodged them.

"I'm gonna kill you!" Al said, over and over, in between punches.

George could not keep dodging for long. Sooner or later, a hit would connect. Eventually, it happened. A wild blow from Al's left fist knocked George sideways. The pain was immense, and George felt blood. He did not have time to dodge another strike.

Al hit George again. This time, George went down. He felt like his whole body was being consumed by fire. Al would not relent. He leaned over the smaller fighter and headbutted him in the face. Blood shot out of George's mouth, covering Al's forehead.

George knew that after one more blow, he'd be out. Perhaps he would die here. Had he chosen the right strategy? Everything depended on exposing Big Jim and exposing him now.

Al stood over George's helpless body,

laughing, rubbing his hands covered in blood. "You die now!" he said.

George braced himself for the end.

"Stop!" someone suddenly said. It was Big Jim. He had stood up without the help of his body man.

"Keep it together, Al!" Big Jim shouted. "You're going to cost me thousands of dollars!"

A second too late, Big Jim realized what he had just said. The game had just been revealed. The audience, already unhappy with the fight, began to get feral.

"Whaddaya mean 'thousands of dollars'?"

"Big Jim, are you playing us? Why did you stop the fight?"

Big Jim tried to explain. "Please, ladies and gentlemen . . ."

"You tried to skim money from *us*? Not even Tweed would do that."

"You're a dead man, Big Jim."

"Get him!"

The crowd tried to attack Big Jim. Al Stevens exited the ring and rushed to his boss's safety. He managed to hold off the angry crowd long enough to escort Big Jim back into his office. The door was locked. Big Jim and Al hid inside. George could faintly hear Big Jim yelling at Al for blowing their scheme.

"Get the police," someone in the audience said.

"They'll be on their way soon," another said.

George was lying in the center of the ring, barely conscious. He could feel loose teeth rattling in his gums. He swallowed his blood and felt the urge to vomit. His limbs ached. He could barely move. But he had won the most important contest: exposing Big Jim. Not only had he won, but he had done so by *not* putting up a fight. As he had always known, violence was not the answer.

In the center of the ring, while an angry crowd ignored him, George managed a smile. Finally, he had a story worth telling.

CHAPTER TWELVE

The next morning's edition of the *New York Times* sold more than any issue since the Tweed bust. The headline was *DICKINSON CAUGHT IN FAKE FIGHT STING*. The byline read *BY HOLLY QUINE*.

George Choogart sat in his room, reading Holly's latest scoop. It would be the last time he would set foot in the small rowhouse apartment that his employer had provided to him. After regaining consciousness, Van Thomas had drawn up papers to remove George from his post. Included in these papers was a warning. George had to stay away from the Times Building and never return. George had never had a chance to write a word for the newspaper. But he had made an impact, despite not writing the words that brought down Big Jim. Even the beaten, bruised Van Thomas would acknowledge this.

Big Jim turned out to be in even more trouble than George had guessed. After his outing in the press, it was revealed that Big Jim had been using the NYPD to hold his political enemies in jail without charges. Among those enemies were Lew Mayflower and the brothers Oakley. The two brothers were finally freed and reunited.

Mayflower in particular used his jail time for all the publicity it was worth. He threatened in the article to testify against Big Jim and invited anyone who was interested to check out "good, clean fights" at the Woodrat. George was glad Lew Mayflower was safe. He was even gladder that the club owner continued to be the same loudmouthed, self-promoting huckster he always was. George knew he would miss Mayflower and the rest of the gang at the Woodrat.

George packed the day's newspaper, his copy of *Bleak House*, and his writ of dismissal in his coat pockets. They were his only possessions. He was about to leave the house when he heard the sound of two women speaking outside his hallway.

"Madam, could you direct me to George Choogart's room?"

"Th' name is Millie, not madam! And George doesn't live here anymore. Wanna hire a haberdasher?"

"Are you telling me there is something wrong with my clothes?" the other woman asked.

"You look like you could use an extra button or two," Millie said.

"Are you accusing me of insufficient modesty?"

"Er . . . yes?"

"I have fought women who accused me of less. You are lucky that today has been such a good day. Now, can you take me to George's room?"

"A cloth, a stitch, some buttons, some ribbons . . ."

"Never mind. I will find it myself."

A few seconds later, Holly Quine walked into George's room. "George, I wanted to thank you."

"For what?" the newly unemployed journalist replied.

"You gave me the scoop of the year and got fired in the process. Why?"

"Big Jim was your beat, not mine," George said. "You said so yourself. Besides, I am glad to be fired. New York is a wonderful city, but it is not for me."

"Really?"

"I grew up in the East End of London. The Bowery is big and colorful and beautiful but also harsh and brutal. I need something new."

"Where will you go next?" Holly asked. "Back to Europe?"

"More like the opposite direction," George said. "I keep hearing stories about the American

West. Vast, untamed wilderness, and the promise of adventure. I think that is where I belong."

"Van Thomas might have disagreed. I saw him, you know. I tried to convince him not to fire you."

"Don't bother," George said. "I didn't belong, so I didn't belong. When you see him again, tell him I'm sorry. Also tell him that he put up a good fight."

"I will."

"I have a train to catch, Holly. I must go."

"West?" she asked.

"Indeed," George said. "Until I see the Pacific."

"Good-bye, George Choogart."

"Good-bye, Holly. You're the best journalist a man could ever hope to read."

"Man *or* woman, Mr. Choogart."

———

George walked to the train station alone, observing his Bowery for the last time. He walked past the flophouses, the theaters, the broken tenements covered in the dust of city life. He saw beggars begging in the street while rich men looked away in shame. Peddlers bothered bystanders, selling their wares. Everywhere George went, he saw life. It was not his home, but it was something to always remember.

The train's engine churned. Gradually, the isle of Manhattan faded into the distance. George was on his way west, traveling deeper into new and undiscovered America.

ABOUT THE AUTHOR

Nathan Sacks is an academic writing instructor and writer who currently lives in Minneapolis, MN. He was born and raised in Ames, IA. His first two books were *American Hip-Hop: Rappers, DJs, and Hard Beats* and *The Duel: Mitsubishi Eclipse*. He enjoys music, reading, and idle daydreaming.

BARE KNUCKLE

AFTER THE DUST SETTLED

The world is over.
Can you survive what's next?